Don't Want to Go!

For Mark

DON'T WANT TO GO!
A BODLEY HEAD BOOK 978 0 370 32962 8

Published in Great Britain by The Bodley Head,
an imprint of Random House Children's Books
A Random House Group Company

This edition published 2010

1 3 5 7 9 10 8 6 4 2

RANDOM HOUSE CHILDREN'S BOOKS
61–63 Uxbridge Road, London W5 5SA

www.kidsatrandomhouse.co.uk
www.rbooks.co.uk

Addresses for companies within The Random House Group Limited can be found at:
www.randomhouse.co.uk/offices.htm

THE RANDOM HOUSE GROUP Limited Reg. No. 954009

A CIP catalogue record for this book is available from the British Library.

Printed and bound in Singapore

Don't Want to Go!

Shirley Hughes

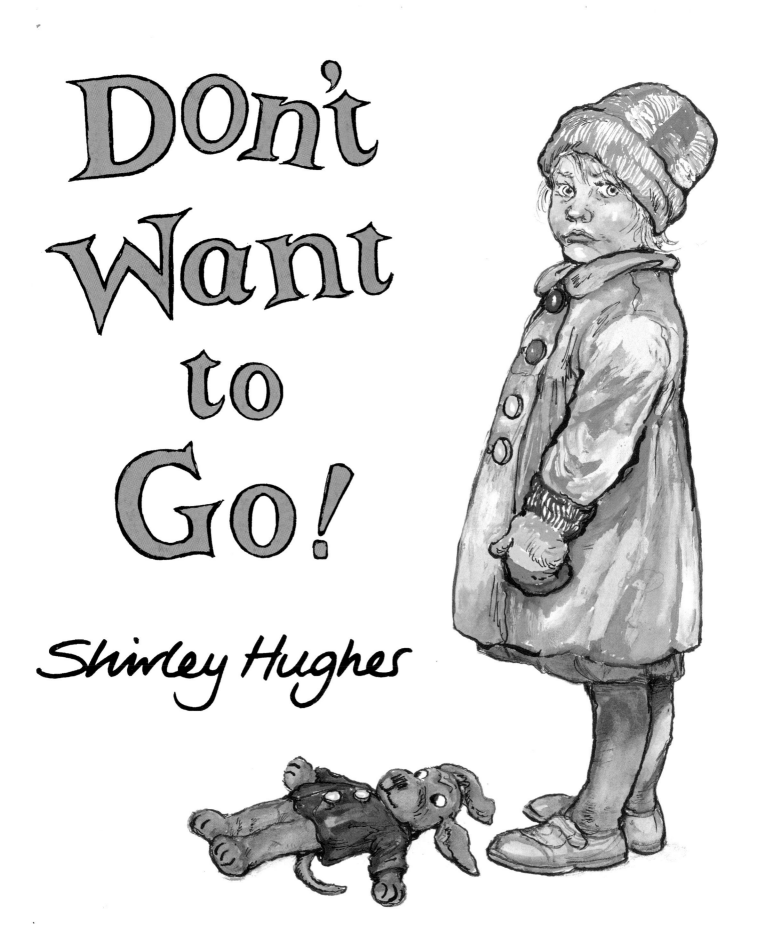

THE BODLEY HEAD

LONDON

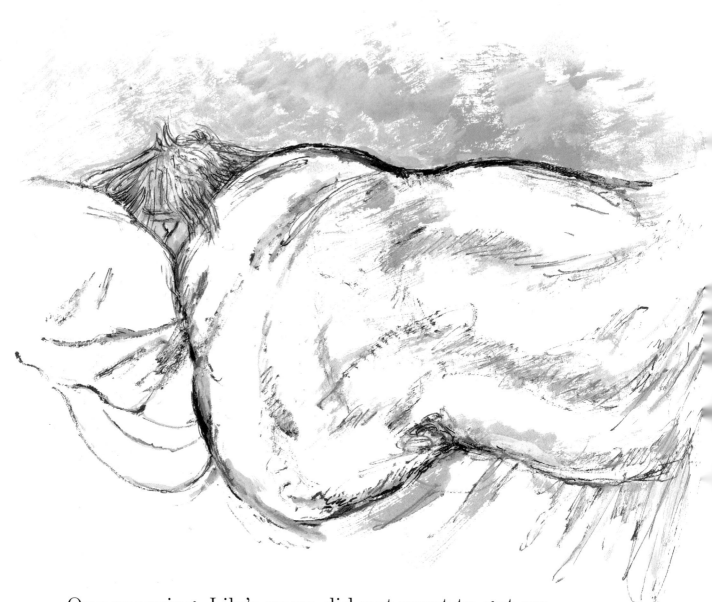

One morning, Lily's mum did not want to get up.
She just lay there with her eyes closed. She said
that her head ached and her throat was sore and
she felt hot and shivery all over.

"Mum has got flu, I'm afraid," Dad said as he gave Lily her breakfast. "She needs to stay in bed today and I have to go to work." He looked worried.

"Who will look after me, then?" Lily wanted to know.

Dad was already speaking on the phone.
When he rang off he said, "Guess what! You're
going to play at Melanie's house!
Won't that be fun?"

"Who's Melanie?" asked Lily.

"You remember Melanie!
You've been to her house
before. She lives just near
here in Wesley Avenue
and she has a big boy
called Jack and
a baby called Sam!"

"I've dropped the
yellow bit of my egg
on the floor," was
all Lily said.

"There'll be lots of nice toys to play with," Dad said. He wiped Lily's mouth and mopped the floor. Then he buttoned her into her jacket and put on her hat and mittens.

"Don't want to go!" said Lily.

"I'll take you in the buggy, it will be quicker," said Dad as he tucked Bobbo in beside her.

"Off we go!" he said in a very jolly voice.

They were just turning into Wesley Avenue when Dad discovered that Lily's mittens were gone.

"I'm sure we put them on before we left the house," he said.

He turned the buggy round.
They were halfway home before
they found the mittens lying on
the pavement.

Dad picked them up and put
them safely back on Lily's hands
again. Then he pushed the buggy
full steam ahead till they reached
Melanie's front door.

It was a yellow door, the colour
of the inside of Lily's egg.

"Here we are!" said Dad.

"Don't want to go!" said Lily.
She went all stiff and would
not get out of the buggy.

But just then the door opened,
and there was Melanie with a
smiling face, holding baby
Sam. He did not have much
hair. He said, "Da!" and held
out his fat little hand to Lily in
a friendly way.

Lily and Dad stepped into Melanie's hall. Lily was clutching Bobbo very tightly. Dad knelt down. He took off Lily's hat and mittens and gave her a big hug. "Have a good time, darling," he said. "I'll finish work early."

"Don't want to stay," said Lily in a tiny voice.

As the door closed on Dad, Lily opened her mouth to give a big yell. But at that moment a little dog ran into the hall. He was white with pale brown ears and patches. He ran straight up to Lily and licked her hand.

Lily liked that. She decided not to yell for the moment after all.

"His name's Ringo," Melanie told her. "And it looks as though he likes you a lot."

They all went into the kitchen. It was warm in there. Ringo's basket was in the corner.

Melanie put Sam in his highchair. "Sam's going to have some toast and honey. Would you like some?" she asked.

"Don't want toast," said Lily. She forgot to say thank you.

While Sam sat in his chair and ate toast and honey, Lily and Bobbo sat under the table.

When Sam had finished, Melanie lifted him out of his highchair and put him on the floor because he was a crawling baby.

Then Sam wanted to play a game of peek-a-boo with Lily.

And Lily couldn't help laughing
because he was so funny.

When Sam was tired, Melanie took him
upstairs for a nap. Then she spread out
some pictures she had cut out of
magazines across the kitchen table.
She fetched some glue and
a big scrapbook.

"Would you like to do
some pasting?" she asked.

"No, thank you," said Lily.

"Well, perhaps you
would like to help
me choose, then,"
said Melanie.

So Lily chose where the different pictures were to go. She chose a piece of cake on a lady's head and a rabbit riding on a fish, a shiny red car in a bed and a building balancing on a chest of drawers. When they had finished, it was a very interesting book.

"You can show it to your dad when he comes to collect you," said Melanie.

Sam was cross when he woke up. He was
crying as Melanie carried him downstairs.
His nose ran, tears trickled down his cheeks
and his mouth was a miserable "O" shape,
showing two tiny teeth.

But when he caught sight of Lily, he
stopped crying, little by little, and began
to hiccup instead.

"He won't do that for me!" said Melanie.
"Thank you, Lily."

At lunch time Lily helped to spoon food into Sam's mouth. A lot went into the wrong places but Sam did not seem to mind.

Soon it was time to pick up Sam's big brother, Jack, from school.

"Don't want to . . ." began Lily.

But Melanie said quickly, "Ringo's coming too and you can help hold his lead if you like."

So Lily held Ringo while
Melanie fixed the lead
onto his collar.

Lily helped to hold onto Ringo all the way to Jack's school.

Sometimes he pulled on the lead and wanted to run ahead so badly that they could hardly keep up with him.

And sometimes he wanted to stop and sniff around.

They all had to run
the last bit very fast
to get there in time.

Ringo went nearly crazy with joy when Jack came running out of school. Jack had curly hair and a beautiful smile with no front teeth.

When they got back, Jack made some cardboard boxes into boats and they pretended that Lily and Sam and Bobbo were sailing far out to sea.

Ringo stayed on the seashore and kept a lookout.

Then they sat together on the sofa and watched television – all except Sam, who played on the floor. Ringo lay between Jack and Lily with his head on Lily's lap.

While they were sitting there, Lily heard the doorbell ring. When Melanie went to answer it, she heard Dad's voice in the hall.

"You've been having a great time, I hear," he said, putting his head round the sitting-room door. "I've come to collect you, as promised."

And he held out Lily's jacket.

But Lily snuggled deeper into the sofa
and hugged Ringo to her chest.

"Don't want to go," she said.